WHEN A KISS

IS NEVER

ENOUGH

de de Cox

Copyright © 2022 by de de Cox

Mr. Mistletoe

All rights reserved. No part of this publication may be reproduced, distributed, or transmitted in any form or by any means, including photocopying, recording, or other electronic or mechanical methods, without the prior written permission of the publisher, except in the case of brief quotations embodied in critical reviews and certain other noncommercial uses permitted by copyright law. For permission requests, write to the publisher, addressed "Attention: Permissions Coordinator," at info@beyondpublishing.net

Quantity sales and special discounts are available on quantity purchases by corporations, associations, and others. For details, contact the publisher at the address above.

Orders by U.S. trade bookstores and wholesalers. Email info@BeyondPublishing.net

CREDITS
Male Model:	Bo Cox
Female Model:	MaKenna Meeks
Photography:	Austin Ozier / Medici Creative
Videography:	Austin Ozier / Medici Creative
Film Trailer/Sizzle:	Austin Ozier / Medici Creative
HMUA/Stylist:	Scooter Minyard
HMUA Assistant:	Jeanette Moore
Wardrobe:	Andre Wilson / Style Icon, LLC
Location:	Nikki / Scenic Hill Equestrian

The Beyond Publishing Speakers Bureau can bring authors to your live event. For more information or to book an event contact the Beyond Publishing Speakers Bureau speak@BeyondPublishing.net

The Author can be reached directly at BeyondPublishing.net

Manufactured and printed in the United States of America distributed globally by BeyondPublishing.net

New York | Los Angeles | London | Sydney

ISBN Softcover: 978-1-637923-74-0

Dedication

In September, my husband and I will celebrate 37 years of marriage. I don't know that we would have ever thought that more than half of our lives in this world would be with each other, but it's true. We eloped (another story). I tease him all the time that I now have benefits in him. I can now receive AARP, Social Security, senior citizens' discounts, and half his "stuff". I always tell folk he's my "trophy husband". We have told both our boys that when you look for a mate (especially, when getting married) find someone who likes the same things and cares about those things you do. They don't have to love those things, but they need to care because YOU care. He loves sports. I do, too. He loves music. I do, too. He is horrible with computer technology. I am, too. Our boys become so aggravated with us when they hear the words "It ain't working, come here, please." He loves bulldogs. I do, too. He didn't like cats, BUT he does now. He is my best friend on a cold wintry day, especially to stay inside and watch football. We can begin with one game and take a nap at halftime AND then wake up for the second game just starting. I am prayerful GOD will grant us 37+ more years together. I love you, Scott Allen Cox – Wifey

Genesis 2:24: Therefore, a man shall leave his father and his mother and hold fast to his wife, and they shall become one flesh.

Introduction

The legend behind kissing under the mistletoe comes from Norse mythology. It is said that there was a god named Baldr. He had a premonition about his death, and he knew he was going to be murdered. His mother, Frigg, was worried about this and made every living thing promise that they would not kill her son. The only thing that she left out was the mistletoe.

Loki, an evil God who knew about this, wanting to exploit this opportunity, attended an assembly in Valhalla, where all the Gods were taking turns in shooting arrows at Baldr for fun; they were in awe when they saw that nothing could harm him. Loki handed Holder, Baldr's blind brother, an arrow made from mistletoe and asked him to take a shot at Loki, too. This arrow killed Baldr.

For three days after his death, every living thing came to revive him but failed. Finally, he was revived by Frigg and the mistletoe, itself. Frigg's tears became little white berries on the mistletoe plant, and she said that anyone who stood under the mistletoe would never be harmed and would be entitled to a kiss. There are many different endings to the legend. One says that Baldr was never revived and was given a Viking's funeral, and people are waiting for him to come back and bring in a new era. But whatever the version, the common fact is that Frigg swore that the mistletoe would never harm anyone and made it a symbol of love. (www.indobase.com)

Chapter One

The incessant ringing of the telephone had set the mood for the morning. This event was going to be the death of her. In less than two weeks, the wedding of the year was taking place. The smallest of details could not be overlooked. She had seen all the reality shows with "those bridezillas". Wren Bailey was praying that this was not the case. She began perusing the checklist. Most items had been completed, but there were a few that remained needing to be confirmed. The last and the most important was the décor for the event.

Wren's partner, Lynette Bailey, who just happened to be Wren's mother, had been given the task for following up with the farm in Brentwood, Tennessee to finalize the delivery date of the décor – the mistletoe. The bride had requested that mistletoe be hung in several strategic spots of the entrance to the wedding reception venue. Wren had visited the church where the wedding was to be held. It was The Basilica of St. Patrick's (one of the oldest churches in New York and possibly the United States). Wren's personal research did not go that far back. Again, Wren prioritized the knowledge needed and then moved on. The church was over two hundred years old. There were fourteen stations of the cross cut in stained glass inside the church. On each side of the pews, seven stations were featured. It took your breath away to see the intricacy and the intimacy attached to HIS walk.

Wren knew this specific wedding would set a precedent for her and her mother's event planning business. The Polished Bannister, LLC was well known in the event planning industry, but this wedding would definitely help with future bookings. Wren and her mother did not attend bridal shows. There was no time. Their business was booked from prior brides' word of mouth and from family who had attended previous weddings Wren had handled. All knew the expertise that Wren and her mother brought to an event.

Walking towards her mother's office, Wren could not help but be a bit nervous. Her stomach was uneasy, and she had no clue why. As she turned the corner, she overheard her mother's voice. Wren had a sixth sense that she could tell if an individual were smiling on the other end or not. Her mother, by all accords of her tone, was not smiling. Wren stood in the middle of the doorway. Watching, as her mother placed the telephone back onto the receiver, and placing her hands on her face and swiping down, Wren knew it was not good news. All she could think to herself was "what now?"

The "what now" was the "order". "Mother, what is it? What's going on with the order?" Lynette Bailey looked at her daughter and quietly in control, stated, "I've just been informed by Mr. Mistletoe that the order cannot be filled. Something to do with the weather and the growth of the mistletoe during the season. To be honest, I'm not sure what the conversation held after the words 'cannot'."

Wren stared at her mother. It was rare for her mother display emotion. She never allowed others to see her reactions. She was in control of the circumstances surrounding her. She had told Wren to never let them see you falter. "For when you do, they see the moment to seize the opportunity of your weakness." Wren had not quite understood the entire implication of the sentence, but as she matured, Wren grew more familiar with the words "in control".

Listening to her mother explain all that had been relayed to her from Mr. Mistletoe, Wren's first thought was, *Who does he think he is? Does he know who he was speaking with? Does he have any clue the amount of business that our company has expended with him in the last year?* Evidently, a telephone call would need to be made as a gentle reminder of the business transactions. Wren needed Mr. Mistletoe to understand the urgency and more specifically, the importance of this wedding. For unknown reasons, Wren was not feeling confident about a telephone call.

Chapter Two

Women! Women in business! Women who owned their own company! This particular woman! Why his dad, Harrison Mistletoe, ever agreed to such a large event was beyond Eliot Mistletoe's comprehension. At this moment in time, Eliot was questioning a lot about this specific booking.

By accident, he had picked the telephone up while walking into the office of the farm. Normally, Eliot's dad, Harrison, would handle the day-to-day office affairs while Eliot would begin the packing and shipping of the mistletoe (all this would be done in another area of the office warehouse). This was not an accident; this was more of a "what the hell just hit me or who just hit me".

Before Eliot could even get "hello" off his lips, which as most country folk knew, was the one obligatory word to begin a conversation, he was cut off with "I don't have time for excuses. We need our order completed. When can we expect delivery?"

No introduction of who was on the other end. No "good morning." Straight and to the point of "her" needs and when "her" needs would be fulfilled. Oh, how Eliot Mistletoe wanted to reply with a sexual innuendo that may knock Ms. Wren Bailey off her high horse, but he didn't. He held back. Tongue in cheek.

He chose the safe route, as many men would do. He let her ramble on until he knew she would need to take a breath to go any further with her tirade. Eliot knew, without a doubt, she was probably an Olympic swimmer. She could probably hold her breath under water for ten minutes or more. What other explanation could there be? That brought a smile to his face. She was like the energizer bunny. She just kept going and going. Was she ever going to shut up?

After she inhaled, Eliot began with the words, "May I speak now?" Her silence was enough confirmation. "Ms. Bailey, I understand that there may have been some miscommunication regarding your order of mistletoe for the event you have scheduled in December. Through no fault of the Mistletoe Farm, the order cannot be filled per the invoice. Due to the dry weather this season, our trees have not produced the mistletoe necessary to fill several of our orders in the latter part of the holiday season. You, Ms. Bailey, are not the only one in a pickle. The Mistletoe Farm is very disappointed it cannot fulfill your order, but I am sure you can understand the predicament we have been placed in. We have no control over the weather or how it will affect our season. Is there anything else that I can do for you, Ms. Bailey?"

Silence. There was no breathing. There was no inhale of a breath. Just complete silence. Before he could ask if she were still there, the disconnection occurred. Not even a "thank you" or "this is unacceptable" or "have a good day." Their world no longer connected. Eliot did not know if he should breathe a sigh of relief or count his blessings that he would no longer would have to deal with this elitest event planner.

His dad walked in. "Who was that? I could hear your conversation all the way to my office. It did not sound like you came to an amicable agreement with Ms. Bailey. You do realize, Eliot, they are one of our most substantial clients when it comes to orders for the holiday season?"

Eliot rolled his eyes at his dad. "Well, I'm pretty sure that is not going to happen this year. I'll make amends in a few days. I'll call and talk to the other owner, Lynette. Maybe she will be much more empathetic than Ms. Wren Bailey. Dad, let's just see what other orders need to be shipped today and get them off the warehouse floor. Tomorrow is a new day and another day for The Mistletoe Farm."

Chapter Three

Done. She was done. She marched down the hallway and straight to her mother's office. "He told me, no. He told me it was not going to happen. He told me something about a "pickle". This man is so infuriating. I hate him and this stupid, little twig. It drives half of the décor for us from October – January. Who? Who invented mistletoe? And why on earth, couldn't this branch of a twig grow in the ground and *not* from a tree?"

Lynette began to laugh. She knew her daughter was a tad bit stressed. She knew these next few months were the critical months for The Polished Bannister and future bookings. What she could not comprehend was how Wren went from ordering mistletoe to the topic of a pickle. A fly on the wall listening to this conversation would have fallen off from laughing so hard.

"Mother, you're laughing. This is not the time. This is our largest wedding of, not just the year, but of the holiday season. We *must* have the mistletoe. There are no ifs, ands, or buts. We will have the mistletoe for the Kennedy wedding. I will *not* accept anything less."

Lynette smiled at her only child. If only her father could see her. She was more like him. She was determined, and she would not let anything or anyone hold her back. In Wren's book, there were no excuses. Excuses were easy. Commitment was what was needed. Lynette valued that characteristic in Wren's father. If he had listened to all the negativity and the naysayers in the industry, The Polished Bannister would never have been founded. The Polished Bannister was not Lynette's dream. It was Wren's and her father's. The goal was to become the largest, the best, the most elite of event planners. It would have come to fruition sooner if he had not unexpectedly passed. Wren was on the cusp of being nationally known. Wren had given herself a timeframe to be number one in two years in the event planning industry. It was happening. Wren would not speak of the disease that had taken her father. She rarely allowed others to see her emotions, but Lynette knew she missed him.

Lynette looked at her daughter. There was only one thing that would jar Wren out of being so mad and stewing. "Well, if I were you, and I am not, but if I were, I would drive to The Mistletoe Farm in Tennessee and check the mistletoe shortage out for myself. But remember, I am *not* you."

Lynette watched her daughter as the wheels began to turn. She could see Wren was weighing the options of something so far-fetched as making a road trip to the country. A road trip that she would be making all by herself. A road trip that consisted of approximately fourteen hours. She waited until Wren smiled a cheeky grin. Lynette knew what was about to happen.

Chapter Four

"Mother, please come check my figures and let me know if I have written down and considered all that I need to do for the trip." Lynette walked in. "Here, let me take a look, honey."

Two pieces of paper lay on the table.

One read:
FLIGHT AND RENTAL – approximately $2,300

The second read:
RENTAL OF COMMERCIAL VAN AND DRIVE UNTIL I PASS OUT – approximately $3,200

Lynette reviewed the numbers. This child needed a vacation. Always exact on any calculations, Lynette knew she did not need to doublecheck the figures. Her main concern was whether Wren could drive the total of 28 hours round trip.

"You are correct. No matter which you choose, the rental of the commercial van is key for this trip in order to return with our order of mistletoe. You can possibly do four hours at a time. Look for a rest area. Pull over and stretch your legs. Then look for a hotel until the morning. I do not want you falling asleep at the wheel, honey."

Wren knew her mother was right on all accounts. If anything, her mother was not just practical, but also sensible. Wren knew she could drive seven hours straight. That was not the concern. The problem was driving fourteen hours straight.

She nodded. "You are right, mother. Both you and I know my capacity to complete a job when I know the deadline we have and what is at stake – our reputation personally, as well as The Polished Bannister's reputation. I'll begin the preparations to leave in the morning. We have four days until the wedding. Trust me, Mother, I can do this. One way or another, there will be mistletoe at the Kennedy wedding come this Saturday."

Lynette smiled at her only child. If anything, Wren was determined. The Polished Bannister was all Wren's idea. Lynette knew she was the support. She had watched Wren work long hours, sometimes into the wee hours of the morning. She observed the weekends that Wren had given up to attend special events with her friends. At those times, Lynette could see how it affected Wren. She was a loner. She preferred to be alone. Wren would repeat time and time again that if Wren were responsible then it was only up to Wren. There could be no failure. Wren would not allow it.

She was too much like her father. Many of Wren's friends would comment that there needed to be time for her to play or at least to enjoy life. She would shake her head no. There was always someone who needed something. Lynette knew had it not been for Wren, the success of The Polished Bannister would not exist. Lynette was grateful for Wren's work ethic.

Listening to Wren's footsteps, Lynette could tell packing was almost complete. She walked towards Wren's bedroom. She could hear her mentally talking to herself. The checklist. Wren never travelled without her briefcase, her calendar, and a notebook, which always held a checklist for an event.

Lynette cleared her throat. "Everything good? Do you need anything from me? The credit card, extra cash, or help with any last-minute event details while you are gone?"

Wren loved her mother. Her mother was the calm in a storm. She was the quiet in the dark. Wren strived to be more like her mother – a woman who exhibited happiness and serenity in all circumstances and who could see the good in any situation. It was at this moment, with this event, and this Mr. Mistletoe that Wren prayed she could exude at least one of these traits.

It was doubtful, but she would do her best. Maybe the drive to The Mistletoe Farm would take away any anxiety that Wren was feeling. Surprises took place every day. Wren rolled her eyes. Wasn't going to happen. Was not going to even come close to the frustration she felt towards Mr. Mistletoe and the predicament he had placed her, her mother, and her business in. It was a good afterthought, though.

Chapter Five

Driving the back roads, Wren's blood pressure was boiling. She could not believe that she had driven from New York to Tennessee, all because of a little twig whose meaning played such an integral part during this time of year. She had to be insane. There was no other explanation.

Wren had made good timing. She had promised herself not to overdo it. If she became tired or felt her eyes becoming weary, she would pull off at the next exit where hotel locations could be seen, and she could rest for the night. She did not need anything fancy. She just needed somewhere safe to lay her head.

Morning came, and Wren walked to the rental van. It was a good thing the vehicle had a step. Otherwise, Wren would have needed one of those little stools she used to stand on as a child to help her navigate things that were out of her reach. The drive was nothing but magical. The countryside was full of fields that had either held tobacco or soy beans. Some held corn. Wren was not a farmer, but she knew by the sites of the big green John Deere tractors in the fields, that corn was about ready to be picked or plucked or plowed. One of the three. Wren could not get enough of the scenery. There were hardly any cars on the road. This state was so much different than New York. There were no honking horns or expletives of what to do with your vehicle.

As she drew near the city that would be where the farm was located, Wren decided it would be best to get a good night's rest and feel refreshed in the morning. She would be ready to tackle Mr. Mistletoe and his firm answer of "no."

Laying in the bed, Wren was jotting down on the contract that she and her mother had signed with The Mistletoe Farm. There were a few specific points she needed to address with Mr. Mistletoe, and then it hit her. She perused her handwritten notes. It was staring her right in the face. This could work. This was the only solution to her problem.

Wren turned the lights out. She reached for her cell and double-checked to be sure she had plugged it in for charging. She realized she had not taken time to brush her teeth. Wren was a methodical individual. She knew she would not be able to sleep until this last task was completed. She would never get rest if she kept thinking of the "next thing to do".

This was her curse she had been living with. Everything had to be in the right place at the right spot before Wren could feel at ease. Sometimes, she touched the same object ten times before she was satisfied with the placement. Wren smiled. The curse of having OCD was the best thing that could have happened to her. Checking everything three times, sometimes four had put The Polished Bannister on the map as the "ONE" event planning organization that would be sure all was set and in place before the attendees even parked.

She sat on the edge of the bed. Mr. Mistletoe could not argue with the plan that Wren had come up with. It was just too perfect. She lay back and closed her eyes. She knew without a doubt, this could and would happen.

Chapter Six

Wren woke up early. Earlier than the time she had set on the alarm. There was no time to waste. An element of surprise was the best way to tackle the issue at hand. But was the issue the lack of mistletoe or Mr. Mistletoe, himself, she asked herself.

Wren showered and looked at the red jacket dress she had chosen for this morning's surprise meeting. She had her high heels laid out. Wren was petite in height. Working in the event planning industry as long as she had, there were a few hidden secrets that had been shared by others. One was the advantage of a level playing field when it came to height. She knew she needed to be eye-to-eye with Mr. Mistletoe to get her point across.

Fastening her seatbelt, Wren did a quick review that she had all the ammunition required where the word "no" would not leave Mr. Mistletoe's lips.

She was less than twenty minutes, according to the GPS, from her destination. She could not fathom why this one conversation had ruffled Wren's feathers, but it had. At this point in the drive, Wren's feathers were not her true worry. How in the world would she make this man, "Mr. Mistletoe", see that the order *must* be fulfilled? Wren was not leaving that farm without her mistletoe.

The morning mist was his favorite time to walk the line of the trees. He walked by each tree to double check the growth and extension of the mistletoe. Even though the farm had encountered a shortage and several orders had to be delayed, the end of the year was coming together. Eliot knew this was a huge accomplishment. Both he and his dad could breathe a sigh of relief, except for that one telephone call.

Eliot could only imagine what this woman on the other end of the phone looked like. If she were anything like her attitude, God probably would have hung upon her, too. He did remember that he had promised his dad that he would call the other owner to make amends. What was her name? Oh yeah, Lynnette.

Walking towards the office, the smoke caught Eliot off guard. It was in a perfect straight line. Eliot knew it was not a fire. If it were a fire, his father had better be yelling for help. There was no smell attached to clouds.

He heard the vehicle approach more than he saw it. He asked himself, *Today was Tuesday, correct?* He did not recall that the farm had any appointments. Whoever was driving the truck was squalling tires and throwing up the rock gravel to the entrance to the farm. This was where the smoke was coming from. He watched as the truck came to a squealing stop less than ten feet from where he was standing. His heart began to race for no reason. He laughed to himself. This could be because the driver behind the wheel was just about to hit him. As soon as he could see the outline of the driver, Eliot muttered to himself, "Oh hell no!"

Eliot could not wait to meet her. He folded his arms across his chest and took the stance. He was not moving, budging, nor repositioning himself. He didn't care if she parked the vehicle on his toes.

Wren saw him. He had his arms crossed. He was standing stark still – like a Roman statute. The stance he posed looked as if he were a Roman god. This made her even more upset. She knew it was him. Who else could it be? It was the owner of The Mistletoe Farm.

Eliot could not help but tilt his head. He was never surprised. But this. He thought this day would just be "normal". By the noise of the truck door being flung open, there was no way this day was going to be "normal". A pair of black high-heeled shoes emerged from the truck and steadied themselves on the gravel.

Curiosity was going to get the better of him. He knew she may need help, but he just couldn't do it. She was the one who was wearing high heel shoes to farm. Eliot shook his head. Most, if not all, of The Mistletoe Farm clients and customers knew to wear casual attire with boots for walking through the fence rows and touring the farm. If picking up an order, they knew to have a heavy jacket or some type of layering across their chest and gloves on their hands, so as not to get scratched. Eliot grinned. This normal day had disappeared up in smoke. This was going to be a great day.

Chapter Seven

The holidays were always full of surprises. This was what Eliot and his dad loved about the holidays. Cherished memories by having customers come back year after year and seeing how their families had grown or lives changed, was what the holidays were meant to be.

There was no doubt that this day was going to be rather intriguing. He watched as the young lady turned to reach inside the SUV and pull out a briefcase. Okay, she was not going to be a fun, let's waste a few moments getting acquainted appointment. You could always tell by a customer's mannerisms how to address their need. This appointment was a no-smile, I don't have the time for pleasantries kind of appointment. Eliot could tell by the way she was walking towards him; this conversation was going to be unpleasant. How quickly could he hand her off to his father to deal with any questions.

As he turned to holler for his father, she cleared her throat. "I can guess since you have not moved and you have been observing me this entire time that you are not a patron of the farm, but the owner?"

The first thought that came to Eliot was that she would chew his dad up as dessert and then look to him as the main course. He just needed to get rid of her. But how? She was getting under his skin. Eliot did not like the way he was feeling. A weird fluttering with his heart had begun. She was way out of her element on the farm, and the state, too, just based on her appearance. He needed to bring her down a notch or two.

"There are two owners of the farm. I am one. The other is my dad. Who do you wish to speak to?"

Wren heard the word "two". Two owners. Who had her mother been dealing with? Her mother had never informed Wren that there were two owners to The Mistletoe Farm. Wren would have remembered.

"I'm sorry, please let me introduce myself. I am, Wren Bailey, the owner of The Polished Bannister from New York. I could be wrong in my assumption, but I think you and I have had a conversation regarding my company's mistletoe order."

Eliot nodded in agreement. "No ma'am, your assumption is correct. It was definitely me. Your memory is spot on." Eliot knew he had caught her attention by saying "no ma'am". Guessing by how her eyebrowed raised, she had never been called "ma'am".

Wren waved her hand in the air. "Yes, yes, my memory, the conversation. My time, Mr. Mistletoe, is not my own these days. The holidays, as you know, especially with weddings and galas for the New Year, have consumed my life. If I could just pick up the mistletoe I ordered for this weekend's event, I will be on the road before "oh, what is that old saying that is coined as a country phrase?"

Eliot could not help it. He laughed. "I'm pretty sure you are referring to "before you can say lickety split".

Wren was not sure if he was being sincere. She could not let Mr. Mistletoe have the upper hand or the last word. According to Wren's mother, this was one of Wren's weaknesses. Not being able to let go. Holding on tight to it. Wren personally felt this was a strength. Particularly, dealing with individuals in the wedding and event planning industry. And, as always, Wren jumped in with both feet or heels, as her case may be, without thinking of the repercussions. "Are you making fun of me, Mr. Mistletoe?"

Eliot was taken back. Feisty was the first word that came to his mind. The first image that entered Eliot's mind was that Ms. Bailey just needed to be kissed into tomorrow, but he chose the safe route. "No, Ms. Bailey. I'm just here to educate you on the proper sayings of the south." Then he winked at Wren.

A wink! He winked at her? Okay. Enough was enough. She still did know about the mistletoe. She was standing on rock gravel in high heel shoes. She had not met the "other owner", and she was exhausted. Why? Where was the dad? At this stage of the game, Wren didn't give three flips. She disliked this Mr. Mistletoe. She would return to New York without the mistletoe.

Chapter Eight

Eliot observed all the emotions taking place. He could tell she was tired. Just the placement of the briefcase on the rock road was a dead give-away. Before he could make amends, Eliot sensed rather than heard, his dad's footsteps walking towards them.

Eliot turned, as his dad *always* hugged him upon greeting Eliot for the day. Before he could caution his dad, he had already walked over and hugged Ms. Bailey. Eliot was waiting for her to back away, but instead, she took Eliot by surprise. She leaned into his dad's warm embrace of welcome. Eliot watched as she let her guard down. She did not have those brows furrowed. Hell, she even smiled as she laid her head to his dad's shoulder.

Eliot shook his head. Well, she was just full of surprises. Eliot watched the exchange. He heard his dad begin with, "We are so sorry we could not ship the mistletoe, but I think I have come up with a plan so that all are happy and the relationship is kept intact. Would you mind coming to the office with me? You can take those high falootin' shoes off and rest a spell while I tell you all about *my* plan. Trust me, it wasn't his." He pointed to Eliot.

Wren had never felt so welcomed by someone she had never met until now. When he reached for Wren and pulled her in for a hug, it was as if her dad were comforting her as he did when she was a little girl. Wren missed her father's hugs. Even though a tough businessman, there had never been a day, he had not freely given hugs to her and her mother. His logic behind a hug was even the most angered, the most upset, the most snot-nosed couple would melt with a hug. To Wren's disbelief, it worked. She had seen it first-hand. She missed her dad. This hug was just what she needed.

Magic. His dad was magic. Eliot watched as he took Ms. Bailey's briefcase and her purse and began to carry both to its destination. There was only one option for Ms. Bailey to do – follow his dad.

Harrison Mistletoe liked this young lady. She was professionally dressed. Her briefcase and purse matched. Her smile was genuine. The best part was she had now cowered to his son's display of teasing. As

Harrison grabbed for the door knob, he was met by Eliot's hand. "I've got this, Dad. We wouldn't want Ms. Bailey to take a misstep in those heels and possibly fall and scruff up her pretty knees."

Wren heard the derision in his voice. She did not want to give him the satisfaction that it had wounded her a bit. She was not some damsel in distress. And if she fell, she would not seek help from him.

"I can assure you Mr. Mistletoe, I can walk in these shoes and some even higher than the ones I am wearing. If I fall, I will pick myself up, wipe off the dirt and gravel and begin again. If you think I'm fragile, you, Mr. Mistletoe, are sorely mistaken."

Wren took a step to enter the office. She knew before it happened. Her right heel had hit an indentation in the gravel and threw her off balance. Without any intention, she fell into Eliot Mistletoe's chest. Her hands reached for his chest to stop her fall. His chest was hard and muscular.

Eliot caught her elbows, so she would not knock them both the ground. "Steady now. We wouldn't want you scuffing up those beautiful heels. I'll bet you paid quite a bit of money for them."

Wren knew he was going to make some kind of snide comment. All morning long, he had been making innuendos about her wardrobe, her heels, her matching purse and briefcase. Enough was enough. She should not have done it, but she did. She looked up into his face. That was her first mistake. Her second mistake, she knew, was she did not turn away from him looking at her. She inhaled. His scent was that of mistletoe.

Eliot realized holding her so close was not a good choice. What was even worse is when she looked at him, he could not take his eyes off her pouty lips. They were perfect for kissing. *Snap out of it!* In his lifetime of dating, Eliot had never felt this magnetism or draw to another. She was mesmerizing. He slid his hands down her arms in order to push her back from his chest. Was he placing her feet on solid ground or steadying himself? Either way, something had just passed between him and Ms. Bailey. Who would make the next move?

Chapter Nine

Wren tried to step backwards out of his embrace. It was not working. The heels. She should never have worn heels to a farm. What was she thinking? It was him. He was still holding her. Wren tried to wriggle her body to free herself of his muscular arms steadying her. That was not working either. The more she wriggled, the tighter he held her.

Eliot could not help but laugh. What was it with the female persuasion, especially those from the city, and high heel shoes? There was always a chance of breaking a leg, rolling an ankle, stepping sideways, or even more so, just walking right out of them. Eliot had seen that happen on more than one occasion.

"Ms. Bailey, stand still, or both you and I are going to tumble to the ground. I do not want you to get that pretty suit stained," Eliot stated.

Wren had enough of him calling her "Ms. Bailey". He was doing it on purpose. It was irritating her, and he knew it. "Okay, enough with the Ms. Bailey. My name is Wren. Please, call me Wren."

Eliot nodded. It was a unique name. It suited her. "Well, then, Wren, let me reiterate one more time. If you do not stand still, we are both going to be in a predicament on the gravel. I suggest you take both your heels off and come into the office. The floor is not so bumpy, nor are there any crannies that might cause you to stumble. Sound good to you?"

Wren knew he was right. He knew he was right, and she hated that he knew he was right. She was getting nowhere with her mistletoe order. Wren did not want to give him the satisfaction, but knowing her luck, she would twist her ankle or break something. She did not need that. Busy season would kick off for the holidays for The Polished Bannister in two weeks, to be exact.

Harrison had been observing the entire exchange of words and looks. He listened as his son baited the beautiful young lady. He was not worried. But his son should be. Harrison cleared his throat to grab their attention. "Have you two finished flirting with each other? Do you need a few more minutes? Just let me know when you are ready, and we can begin. I'll just wait over here, behind my desk."

Both Wren and Eliot looked at each other and then at Eliot's dad. "Mr. Mistletoe, please let me apologize. I am not one to waste time. Especially when it comes to my business," Wren stated with sincerity.

Harrison smiled. "I agree with you, Ms. Bailey. I don't like wasting time either. I know you have driven a very long way. Let's see what we can do to get your order filled and get you back on the road. Oh, and one more thing, you may want to call your mother. She's called here twice to see if you arrived at the farm."

Wren inhaled and left out a deep breath. Her mother. In all the chaos taking place in the drive up the rock road, Wren had forgotten to call her mother. She would be livid. This would take additional time to explain to her mother why she was not on the road back to New York.

Harrison saw the concern pass over her face. "I tell you what, Eliot and I will step outside and give you some privacy. Go ahead and place that call to your mother. When you have relayed to your mother that you are still alive and breathing and at The Mistletoe Farm, just open the door and holler for us. We'll come right back." Harrison gave her a nod of his head and wink to let her know he understood that she needed to do this first.

Wren pursed her lips together. This morning was not going as planned, but she knew her mother would be anxious about her safety and her location. "Thank you, Mr. Mistletoe. I will not be long."

Eliot turned and held the door for his dad. Walking back outside, Eliot knew he was going to get the "spill". Eliot knew he had been egging and teasing Wren and from the looks of the eyebrows of his dad, he did, as well.

"Eliot Mistletoe, what in the world has gotten into you? Mind your manners, and leave the young lady alone. She's probably tired from the drive and frustrated about her order. Quit being a jackass."

Eliot stopped in his tracks. His dad never took up for any women clients that had laid foot-prints on the farm. Why was he doing it now? Something was wrong.

"Dad, she can handle herself. Look what she drove up in. Look at what she is wearing. Her briefcase, alone, costs more than our home. She's definitely an only child. She probably gets everything she wants or desires," Eliot stated with derision.

Harrison looked at his only child. "Play nice, son. I like her, and if looks are deceiving, so do you. The Polished Bannister is a huge client and has been with us for over fifteen years. I don't want to lose their business."

Chapter Ten

As Wren ended the telephone call with her mother, anxiety began to set in. Where had this morning gone? All she needed was the mistletoe. Was that too much to ask for? Just to complete her order. She opened the door and walked back outside. She saw both father and son standing with their backs to her. The discussion seemed quite intent as she saw Eliot's father place his hand on Eliot's arm, as if to forewarn or caution him.

Wren had overheard the words "play nice" and placed her hand to her mouth to cover her giggle. She observed Eliot from behind. It was a hunch, but she knew Eliot Mistletoe didn't "play nice" with anything or anyone.

Wren was trying not to disturb their conversation, but with her high heels and the rocks and the crunching noise, she could not hide the fact she was walking towards them. At the exact moment she stopped a few feet away, both men turned around. One was smiling. One was not. Wren knew why the one was not smiling. But the other was beaming from ear to ear, as if he were about to convey a hidden secret or surprise.

Eliot twisted his head to look at his dad with a smirk. Why was this particular woman getting under Eliot's skin? Why was his dad so taken with her? The sooner he got Wren Bailey off his property and headed back to New York, the better.

Wren felt uneasy. Depending on which one spoke first, she knew this would determine the outcome of her trip. Before she could question any more motives of Eliot Mistletoe, Harrison began his sentence with, "Ms. Bailey, I know that we can help you. If you can give my son and me until the end of the day, which would be around 5:00 p.m., we will have you loaded and ready to head back to the Big Apple. Is this okay with you?"

Wren's mouth dropped, and she began to laugh uncontrollably. From the looks of Mr. Mistletoe and Eliot, they probably thought she may need medication or something to eat, possibly both. "Mr. Mistletoe, I'm so sorry. I didn't mean to laugh at your statement. I thought you were going to tell me the worst-case scenario. I am ecstatic and relieved at the same time."

Wren observed Eliot. He smiled. It was a real smile. She had not seen him smile all morning. It was genuine. He looked directly at her. "Wren Bailey, looks like your wish has come true. You will have that mistletoe. So, if I were you, and I'm pretty sure I already know the answer to this, I'd be changing clothes, so we can get to work with your mistletoe order. You do have a change of clothes and shoes, other than high heels, that you can change into?"

Wren wanted him to know how much she appreciated their kindness. She couldn't help but place her hand over eyebrow in a salute and with the words "Aye, aye, Captain Mistletoe."

Chapter Eleven

Wren had changed in the office. She was a bit hesitant to walk out and hear the comments from Eliot, but she did not have time to think about him or her wardrobe. She needed to be on the road at a certain time. While in the office, she had called her mother and informed her of all that transpired.

She looked at herself in the office bathroom mirror. If she were back in New York, there was no doubt in her mind that her friends would take a second look and wonder where their "city" friend had disappeared to.

Wren had changed into her hiking boots, jeans, long sleeve thermal shirt, and her favorite jean jacket. Shoot, she could be a part of the Mistletoe family. She looked every bit the part. She smiled. She didn't mind this casual look. If she were admitting anything to herself, she enjoyed the casual look. Due to the industry, she was always dressed to the nines or possibly, even tens, depending on the event.

She stepped back. Quit stalling. Just go outside. You know he's already going to make a comment. He had been all morning. Why would he change now? A deep breath and out the office door she walked towards father and son. Her boots crunched more against the gravel rock than her high heel shoes. It gave warning to everyone within a ten-mile radius, especially, him, of her arrival.

She watched as he turned towards the very now familiar noise – her. She shook her head. There was no way on this farm she could be quiet or even try to sneak upon anyone. Just go ahead and face him.

Something was wrong. Eliot was not walking towards her. Instead, it was Eliot's father. He stopped. "Ms. Bailey, you are loaded up. The entire order has been completed. You are ready to get back on the road and head home. There is one little hiccup. It's nothing to worry about. It's just that I would prefer you not drive back alone. I've asked Eliot if he would accompany you. He will help unload the order and assist with the set up. Once all has been completed to your satisfaction, Eliot will fly home."

Wren's eyes grew wide. Not with enthusiasm that the order was filled, but more with the fact that she would not be alone returning to New York. "Mr. Mistletoe, I can assure you I am quite capable of driving back to New York all on my own. I did drive here by myself."

"Yes, you did. But you have not had adequate time to rest. And to turn around in less than eight hours and make the trip again, I am adamant that Eliot make the journey with you."

Eliot laughed. Wren turned to face Eliot. She had yet to hear him make that sound. Laughter. She didn't think he was capable of showing this emotion. She twisted her head and asked, "Would you care to share with me what is so funny?"

"I'm not laughing at you, Wren. I'm laughing because you are trying to figure out how to get out of this predicament. My dad will not give in. I will be riding back with you. You might as well just agree with him, so we can get on the road," Eliot informed her.

Wren placed her hand across her lips. She could not help but let a small giggle out. She just needed to get back. She needed to return to her home. She needed her mother. Wren threw her hands up. "I give. I give. Whatever it will take for me to get this mistletoe back in time for the wedding, I will do. I cannot for the life of me, Eliot, fathom why I'm agreeable to do this, but my intuitive instincts tell me you are a man of your word and I'm in safe hands."

Wren watched as Eliot's father hugged him and patted him on the back. She heard Mr. Mistletoe whisper loudly to his son, "Please don't tick her off. I know how you can be when put in a situation you do not want to be in. Just play nice. Okay, son?"

Eliot grinned. "Dad, have a bit of faith in me. I promise to play very nice. I will be sure to take care of all her needs."

Harrison Bailey gave his only son a direct look, "And that's what worries me."

Chapter Twelve

Wren did not want to look over. First, she could not believe he agreed to her driving. Second, she didn't trust Eliot Bailey. Something about that cheeky grin of his set alarms off in Wren's body. She did not want him to know she was thinking about him. She was intimidated by his closeness to her in the SUV. Why in the world she was nervous was beyond her. *Don't look. Don't turn. Don't even move your eyes to the side. Just drive. Focus on the road.* Her heart was racing. There was no good reason for this except him.

Wren was always in control. This was why The Polished Bannister had the reputation it did within the industry. Wren and her mother had worked hard to establish and build the business. Wren had met local celebrities as well as the rich and famous and was never at a loss for words or uneasy when meeting new connections. What hold did Eliot Mistletoe have over her?

Eliot could sense her uneasiness. You could cut the tension in the air with a knife. He was afraid to shift his position in the seat. He did not want to travel over ten hours with Wren and not at least get to know a bit about her. There had to be something in common he had with her. Before he could change his mind, he thought to himself, *The worst that can happen is the entire journey will be silence.* So, he stated, without looking at her, "So, tell me about the wedding that has your feathers ruffled."

Wren burst out laughing. "My what ruffled?"

"Your feathers, Ms. Bailey. What is so important about this wedding that you drove all this way and now, a complete stranger is riding with you to help you set up for this wedding. What is it about this wedding, this particular wedding, that has ruffled you?"

Wren did look at him. That was a mistake. In that close proximity, she could see the color of his eyes. Deep, dark blue. They were the color of a storm on a hot summer night. "We agreed back at the farm for you to call me Wren, and I'll call you Eliot. There's no need for formalities. I'm sure we will be sharing small talk on our way back. Agree?"

Eliot nodded. "Agreed. So let's share. Tell me about this event. What is so unique about this wedding? We have at least ten hours to discuss."

Wren felt Eliot's sincerity. She began the details of how this wedding would become the pinnacle of her career and set the precedence for future events. From the first moment she had spoken to the Kennedy family for the initial consultation until the last meeting of final details, specifically, geared around the mistletoe, Wren and her mother were aware of the importance of this wedding and the doors that would be opened.

Eliot's laugh was warm. Wren suddenly realized she had not taken a breath since beginning the story of the Kennedy wedding and the significance of this little twig.

Wren smiled in return. "I'm sorry. I could not help myself. I get rather lost in my conversation when I am excited about an event. It's like no other feeling I can describe. It's such an exhilaration of life."

Eliot nodded. "I understand. Both dad and I can feel the spirit of the Christmas holidays when the mistletoe farm is at peak season with visitors and customers. It's a natural high."

So, he did understand her enthusiasm. Wren wanted to know more about Eliot Mistletoe. She knew, just as he made the observation, they were going to be in close quarters for well over ten hours. There was no better opportunity than this moment.

"Eliot, since we do have several hours to get to know each other, can I ask you a few personal questions?" Wren waited.

Eliot could sense she was trying to break the ice. It was going to be a long drive. He did not want to drive in silence. He was enjoying her company. "Sure, why not. Just so you know, I'm not good at formal interviews. But go ahead and fire away." Eliot winked.

Wren liked his sense of humor. She felt at ease with Eliot. "Why did you ever go into mistletoe farming? You can only do the Christmas holiday. Typically, your time frame is the week of Thanksgiving until New Year's Eve."

Eliot knew she was taking her time wording the question. He had been asked this question so many times, and the answer had and would always remain the same. "Wren, my dad and mom started the business. They were partners in everything that they did. We lost my mom when I was in high school. My dad needed the help. He did not ask me. I did not ask him. I did what needed to be done. All the success I have achieved is in part to him and that berry. There were struggles, of course, but there was never a time that I wanted to walk away. The holidays really do not play as much importance as you think. The farm has an on-line store for other products to be purchased throughout the year. Yes, the holidays do bring in the most dollars for the farm. When it comes to thinking outside the box for the farm, we are multi-faceted."

Wren did not hear anything else after the words "we lost my mom." They had more in common than Eliot knew. "Thank you for sharing, Eliot."

"Now, Miss Wren Bailey, I want to ask you a question or two. You use this twig or berry in your events and galas during the holiday season, but do you truly know the story of mistletoe?"

Wren turned to look at Eliot. No. She did not. She had never researched about mistletoe other than to know that Eliot's farm was the supplier for the Polished Bannister and events. "No, I can honestly say I never thought about researching mistletoe. When I needed it, The Mistletoe Farm supplied, and no questions were ever asked. Oh, I saw the invoices, but I had no idea about how vast the farm truly was. Plus, the holidays are romantic, and everyone wants to be kissed during the holidays. That little berry just makes it easier without all the worry. Tradition says you're going to be kissed if you stand under the mistletoe."

"Well, let's educate you on this berry. So long as you do not get sick while I'm driving, we are good. Go ahead and pull your cell phone out. Google the words 'story of mistletoe'. Let me know when you find it."

Wren pulled her cell phone out. She began typing. "Found it."

Eliot said in a soft tone. "Read to me, Wren. Read to me the story of mistletoe."

Wren shivered. Was it anticipation? Was it anxiousness? Why his voice sent shivers down her spine with the words "read to me", she could not explain. She nodded and began.

"Well, since you begged me, I will share the story with you." Eliot's eyes widened. "Begged you. I did no such thing."

Wren waved her hand in the air. "Fine. No begging, you only asked me politely." Eliot could not help it. He laughed. "You're incorrigible. Is this how you are going to behave the entire trip? Remember what my father told me, 'Eliot. Behave.' Eliot winked at Wren. He watched as her cheeks began to blush pink. "Should I be telling you, Miss Bailey, to behave?"

Before she could give Eliot an answer, Wren placed her finger on her lips. "Sssshhhh, I have a story to tell."

> "The story goes that Mistletoe was the sacred plant of Frigga, goddess of love and the mother of Balder, the god of the summer sun. Balder had a dream of death, which greatly alarmed his mother, for should he die, all life on earth would end. To keep this from happening, Frigga went at once to

air, fire, water, earth, and every animal and plant seeking a promise that no harm would come to her son. Balder now could not be hurt by anything on earth or under the earth. But Balder had one enemy, Loki, god of evil, and he knew of one plant that Frigga had overlooked in her quest to keep her son safe. It grew neither on the earth nor under the earth, but on apple and oak trees. It was lowly mistletoe. So, Loki made an arrow tip of the mistletoe and gave to the blind god of winter, Hoder, who shot it, striking Balder dead. The sky paled, and all things in earth and heaven wept for the sun god. For three days, each element tried to bring Balder back to life. He was finally restored by Frigga, the goddess, and his mother. It is said the tears she shed for her son turned into the pearly white berries on the mistletoe plant, and in her joy, Frigga kissed everyone who passed beneath the tree on which it grew. The story ends with a decree that who should ever stand under the humble mistletoe, no harm should befall them, only a kiss, a token of love."

Chapter Thirteen

Eliot watched for her reaction after she finished. He could not help himself. Eliot inquired, "Do you believe the story, Wren? Do you believe that a kiss can save you from harm?"

Reading and grasping the story, Wren could not help but feel alive and vibrant. The story was exhilarating. If she were honest, she had never thought to research the story of this twig that brought magic to the Christmas holidays.

"I don't know, Eliot. To be honest, I've never given it any thought. The story, the meaning, the outcome. I've never been kissed under mistletoe. I'm usually decorating and never have the time to look up. I do place it in strategic places for those individuals that are brave enough to stand under the mistletoe at our holiday events," Wren completed her thoughts out loud.

Eliot grinned. "Wren Bailey, you have so much to learn about this incredible plant and the impact it brings to the individuals who stand under it, all with the intent purpose of being kissed."

Eliot could tell she has absorbed every detail of the story. He loved sharing with customers the story of mistletoe. How something so small could be such a life-changer for those who took the chance, while walking under it, for an opportunity of a kiss.

Without hesitation, Eliot told her that would be an easy fix and he could change that one small fact. Wren could feel her entire body react to his statement. She was going to run off the road if any more comments or innuendos were made about mistletoe and kissing.

Eliot knew she would be drained. She had travelled quite a distance. He admired the fact she had driven the distance all by herself. He did not want her to know that he was impressed by her take charge attitude. Wren removed her right hand from the steering wheel and wiped her eye. Eliot had seen this before. She was trying to stay awake. They needed to find hotel accommodations. It was time to pull into a hotel. How to bring this up with someone as stubborn as Wren would be tricky, but it had to be done. Now, which exit and which hotel?

Checking in Eliot felt that adjoining rooms would be best. He could tell from the twist of her head at his statement, Wren was going to object. "There's no arguing. It's adjoining rooms. I can't see through metal and neither can you." Wren was too exhausted to argue.

As they arrive at their assigned room numbers, Wren stops him. "Eliot, please don't lock the adjoining door. It's not that I am going to need you or anything, but just in case. Okay?" Eliot realized what this request had taken her to ask. "It will remain unlocked Wren, as a just in case situation."

Eliot was laying in the bed, staring at the ceiling. He wondered if she were doing the same. Would her thoughts be so engulfed by the wedding that she would give no thought to him. Eliot got up and walked towards the adjoining door. The door that was unlocked, per Wren's request. This door was the only thing separating them. He reached for the doorknob.

Wren could not get comfortable. She should be doing a last-minute mental check for the wedding. But instead, she was thinking of him. He promised he would not lock the adjoining doors. Maybe she should get up and check that he held true to his word. She couldn't stand it. What if he forgot. She walked toward the door. She placed her hand on the doorknob.

He turned away. He could not. She was more than likely fast asleep. He did not want to disturb her. Walking back to the bed, Eliot shook his head. She was turning his world upside down and inside out. Eliot smiled. Upside down wasn't too bad. Inside out was okay, too. He placed his arm over his head and nodded off.

She stepped back. Wren couldn't help but to wring her hands. What was wrong with her? Why was she so nervous? What was there to be nervous about? Wren stepped away. Either open the door or go to bed she told herself. Wren looked at the bed and then the door one more time. She was not thinking clear. She definitely needed rest. Her head hit the pillow and she knew within seconds she would be out for the night.

Chapter Fourteen

Wren woke to a startling noise. She pulled the covers up tight around her chin. She had no desire to find at this late time in the evening to search where the noise was. Her only thought was, she needed Eliot.

As quiet as a church mouse, she opened the adjoining door. She poked her head in. Wren whispered his name. There was no movement. There was no response from Eliot. She could hear him breathing. Good, he's a sound sleeper. Wren tippy toed across the carpet. Now what? She was standing directly by the bed. Wren imagined the bed shifting and waking Eliot. That definitely was not the plan. She did not want the bed to shift with her weight. There had to be a way that Eliot would have no idea she was in the bed with him. She wanted to feel safe. Ever so gently, Wren placed the cheeks of her butt on the edge of his bed. Okay – she was good so far. Just a few more inches and she would be able to wriggle into his bed, close her eyes and get some rest. Her last thoughts were don't breathe. Not yet, hold your breath. Don't wake him.

He heard her as soon as she opened the door. Eliot waited. Something was wrong. If he asked, she would probably say nothing. So, better to play it safe and act as if he were sound asleep. A snoring effect would probably be too dramatic. Eliot needed to act as if he were just asleep. He could hear her as she approached the bed side. If he moved to allow her in, then she would know he was awake. Oh, how he wanted to make it easier on her to get in bed with him. She was never going to make it from the way she was squirming. She would hit the floor before settling in. This was ridiculous.

Just as Wren was about to lay her body into a straight position onto his bed, he felt the shift of her weight in the bed. "Wren Bailey, stop fussing and trying to figure out to how to get into bed with me." He rolled over so he could see her eyes widen with the fact that he was awake. "Come here. I will not bite. Well, maybe a nibble or two."

He was awake. He was not asleep. She could not move. Her legs were as heavy as a yuletide log. She nodded "no." Then, she felt his arm reach around her waist. She was going to lose her balance if she did not do as he instructed. That would be even worse and more embarrassing than trying to get in bed with him. What a comedy of errors.

As she succumbed to his guiding touch, Eliot spooned her into his chest. "Eliot, I heard a noise and…."

"Wren, sweetheart, shut up and go to sleep. We will deal with the noise in the morning."

Morning came, and Wren knew something was not right. She was in bed with Eliot. Not only that, he was playing with her breast. Her nipple was swollen. She froze. Maybe, just maybe, if she did not respond, he would stop. Wren could not help the moan that escaped her lips. She could not stand the emotions coursing through her body. Her nipple became taut with desire. This was insane. She did not know Eliot Mistletoe. Only 72 hours had passed between them, and here she was brazenly allowing him to arouse her.

Eliot did not know how it happened. When he awoke, he felt her. She had not moved. She remained spooned into his chest. For her, big mistake, huge mistake. For Eliot, it was heaven. He reached his hand around to cup her breast and began the gentle caressing of her nipple. He teased her nipple with the twirling of his fingers. He felt the change in her body. When she inhaled, this gave Eliot more room to explore.

Wren did not want him to know how much his touch was affecting her. Her body was betraying her. She could feel the desire in her lower belly. There was an ache at the core of her being. Wren knew the outcome if she wriggled closer into Eliot. She did not care. She could feel him.

Eliot could only take so much. During the holidays, Eliot did not have time for such pleasures. Especially, one that had literally just fallen into his bed. The holiday hours were long. By the time his day ended, he was wiped. The only scenario Eliot could handle was shower and bed and then to be able to repeat it all over again. This was a gift.

Wren waited for him to release her. He did not. He was not going to release her. Eliot placed his lips along her back. The kisses were light to the touch. She could feel his lips move lightly down the middle of her back until he reached her butt.

"Wren, do you want me to stop?"

Wren could not utter one word. She had been left speechless with the action of his lips. She nodded her head "no" and then, to her surprise, she muttered the words, "Please don't stop, Eliot."

She wanted to tell him that she wanted this. She did not want him to know how much he was affecting her world. Waiting for Eliot's next move, she knew it had been a bit of time since she had been made to feel these emotions. Wren was lightheaded. Eliot was bringing feelings to the surface she thought she had hidden away long ago. Wren had to admit, she had been on autopilot for the past two months. The galas, weddings, and special events were all structured with a fine-tooth comb during the holidays. She gave herself no time to respond to the outside world.

Laying in the bed and feeling Eliot's kisses along her back sent a chill through Wren. He stopped at the back of her thigh and placed his hand on her buttock and began massaging. Wren could only think of the fact that what was taking place in this bed was not structure nor was it structured.

Eliot could not resist. He needed to kiss all of her. From her neck to….the places he could imagine.

He would allow his tongue to lead. Eliot stroked her cheek and kissed her swollen lips. Placing his hands on Wren's lower back, her pulled her closer. Raising his hand up to her long hair, he entangled his fingers in it. Her hair was soft to his touch.

Eliot did not want to rush Wren. He brushed his fingers across her shoulders. Every nerve ending in Wren's body tingled with excitement. Eliot could not help himself. He ran his hand down her body. Looking deep into Wren's eyes, he asked "You do realize I want you?"

Wren looked at Eliot. "I do. I want you, too, Eliot. Please."

They took turns removing each other's clothing. The only remaining thing left between Wren and Eliot was time.

He moved from her throat, down to her collar, and then placing kisses on her breasts. He kissed Wren's stomach. He watched as she took a breath.

Eliot wanted to take time to explore Wren. He loved feeling her twist and turn to accommodate his body.

Eliot's fingers inched further along. Again, exploring Wren's body. Deeper. Lower. Wren gasped in anticipation. "Open yourself to me, Wren."

Wren parted herself for Eliot. She waited for the pain as he entered. There was none. Just an overwhelming desire for him never to leave.

Eliot looked down at her. Her eyes were not closed. They were looking at him. There is such a moment that when two bodies bond as one, there is nothing that can separate the smooth rhythmic motion – not even a split second. Wren Bailey was teaching Eliot that one cannot take pleasure without giving pleasure. She returned every gesture, every caress, and every look back to him.

Eliot knew he would never be able to erase the scent of Wren or the memory of their lovemaking.

Chapter Fifteen

Laying beside him, Wren came to the conclusion she did not want to leave his arms. The Universe was as it should be. She smiled.

He saw. "What are you smiling at?"

"I don't know. I can't help it though."

"It couldn't be me, now could it?"

"No", she giggled, "it has nothing to do with you."

Before he could tease her again, she sat up and swung her legs over the bed.

He knew her entire demeanor had changed in just those few seconds. He watched as her back stiffened against his touch.

She turned to look at him. "We need to get on the road. I'm headed back to my room to shower. I suggest you do the same. I'll meet you downstairs in the lobby to check out."

That was it. That's all she could say. Eliot nodded in agreement. He watched as she stood up, the silhouette of her body as she turned to walk into her room. Good Lord, it was going to be a long quiet morning and probably drive. He hated to admit it. He had never met an enigma like her. One minute hot. One minute cold. Always in control. He smiled. He loved a challenge.

She did not look back. She knew he was watching her. She felt his eyes on her. Any other time, she would feel uncomfortable with this predicament, but she was not. As a matter of fact, she felt warm all over. Before closing the adjoining door behind her, she heard him ask "would you like company?" She dare not turn around for he would see her blushing. "No, Eliot, I can handle everything from here. I'll see you downstairs in the lobby." The door closed.

Standing at the sink, looking at herself in the mirror, Wren did not know who she was. At home, she would never have done a one-night stand, especially with only knowing the guy for less than 72 hours. The thing about that "guy" was she did not feel bad for what had just taken place. Wren did not want him to know or have the satisfaction of knowing she enjoyed herself, way too much.

Peering down at the cell phone and hitting the clock, she needed to call her mother. She had promised her mother that she would call upon arrival at the hotel. Well, that had gone by the wayside. It would be mid-morning before they got on the road. Making the call, she heard her mother answer "How is the trip going? Are you getting along with Mr. Mistletoe? I was expecting a call from you earlier. Why the delay? What do you need from me, honey?"

Wren knew she was not going to be able to convince her mother that everything was going well because Wren's mother could sense when something was amiss. Wren took a deep breath and began, "Mother, when I arrived, he was so mean. His father was very nice. I really liked him. But he made snide comments and off-handed jokes about my wardrobe and heels. To top it off, he decided we needed to check in to a hotel and rest. I didn't need to rest. But I could not persuade him otherwise. And then, one thing led to another. I ended up in his bed. I'm in my room. I just showered.

I need to be sure you contact Kash and let her know we will be arriving late this evening and we need to get to work. Can you do that for me?"

"Wren, breathe, honey, breathe. I heard everything you said, but more importantly, you need to take a breath. And then repeat for me, very slowly, how you ended up in his bed. A bit of clarification would help me see through the clouds." Lynette could not help but smile. It was a blessing that her one and only daughter could not see that smile.

"Mother, I am breathing. I'm talking to you, correct? This is my mother, Lynette Bailey?" Wren questioned with frustration.

Lynette could not hold back the laughter any longer. "Yes, Wren, this is your mother. You only have one, and it's me on the other end of this conversation."

Wren was exasperated at this point. Why couldn't her mother just call Kash? Wren didn't have time to explain everything, just that Kash would be needed upon Wren's arrival back to New York with the mistletoe order and him. "Mother, please, just do as I've asked. Please, no more questions."

"It's already done, Wren. Calm down. I've just texted Kash. She responded she will be here tonight. Are we good? Are there any additional details you may want to divulge before you arrive tonight?"

Wren placed the cell phone down. She knew there was nothing to panic about other than who was adjacent to her hotel room. Her mother and Kash would take charge. The mistletoe would be delivered. The event would take place. The only obstacle in her way was the concern of what to do with him once they arrived. She could not think about this now. She needed to finish getting ready. Getting on the road and back to New York was her priority. *Let's hope he's ready.*

Chapter Sixteen

He could hear her talking. From what little he could hear, she was speaking with her mom. Eliot had showered. He had taken a bit more time than he anticipated, but it was needed. He needed time to prepare himself to face her after the evening's events. He didn't know what he would say. He was not even sure how he was going to approach Miss Wren Bailey with all that took place.

The decision was taken out of his hands. He heard her footsteps as they approached the adjoining doors. He walked towards the door. He was ready to grab the door handle and open, when she pushed open the door and hit him square on the forehead.

"Wren, slow down. I'm right here. What's the rush?" He placed his hand on his forehead. He felt a bit lightheaded. He backed up against the dresser to balance himself.

Wren was appalled. She had almost knocked him out. She immediately approached him and pulled his hand away so she could get a better view. She placed her hand over the knot that was forming. He winced. Oh my lawd, he could have a concussion, and it was all her fault.

Eliot knew that Wren had no idea where she had positioned herself while examining him. She was close enough that Eliot could inhale her scent. She smelled of peppermint. She was like a candy cane, just waiting to be licked and swirled around in your mouth.

Eliot grabbed Wren's hand and pulled it down. He placed his thumb under her chin. "I'm fine. I'm okay. But if you stand much longer in front of me, you will not be. I let you go this morning. There are no guarantees I will do so at this moment. So that we are not late for this evening, my suggestion would be to quickly step away from arms. I promise, I'm good for the trip."

Eliot watched as her face recognized what he was implying. She stepped back with her hands down to her side. He reached for her and with light, feathery, teasing strokes, massaged her arms up and down and looked at Wren and stated with such passion and emotion, "You are lucky we are in crunch time. I can promise you there will be a continuation of last night's events."

Wren could not look at him. He would know how his touch was affecting her. She needed to remain in control and not think about his touch. It would be so easy to give in. She did not want to admit it to herself. From the moment she met Mr. Eliot Mistletoe, her world was turning inside out. She was not used to this. Control and routine and had been thrown out. It was chaos.

She looked at Eliot. "I do understand" was all she could muster.

Eliot touched the side of her face. "Quit worrying. It's going to be just fine. I'm packed. Grab your overnight bag, and let's go."

Eliot placed their bags in the van. "I'll drive. You need to rest, so you are ready to hit the ground running when we arrive. Just exactly where are we headed to?" Eliot smiled.

Wren laughed, too. "I guess having directions would be a benefit. We are headed to the wedding venue. My mother will meet us there. It will be late, but we can unload and then return in the morning to begin set up preparation. The church is Basilica of St. Patrick's."

Wren watched as Eliot punched in the address so it would appear on the screen in the van. He started the van and laid his hand on top of hers and held it. "Take a nap, Wren. If I need you, I will wake you."

Travelling for two days straight and then the meeting with Eliot and his father and turning right back around, she hated to admit it, but she could use the time to close her eyes, if only for a few minutes. She nodded in agreement. She noticed he did not remove his hand from hers. She rather liked it there. It made her feel safe.

Eliot watched her. He did not want to remove his hand until he knew she was resting. He liked where his hand was. He would rather his hand be in her hair or teasing her nipple breast to become taut with desire. That would have to wait though. He was a patient man. Eliot smiled.

He remembered something his dad had told him. "Good things come to those who know what patience is." Eliot would be patient. Wren Bailey was one of the "good things."

Chapter Seventeen

Eliot had arrived at the destination, or at least what the GPS said the destination was. Everyone knew that at times the GPS was a hit or miss depending on new roadways and construction taking place. He pulled into the church parking lot and placed the van in park. He noticed there were cars already parked. This had to be Wren's mother and the crew who were there to help unload.

She had slept the entire way. Eliot did not mind. It gave him time to think about the last 72 hours. How this young lady had affected his life and his family business in just these few short days, he had no idea. She was like a controlled tornado, if that were even possible. He hated to wake her. He reached to touch her.

He squeezed her hand. "Sleeping beauty, time to wake. We are at Basilica of St. Patrick's Church. And it looks like the entire city is waiting to greet you."

Without hesitation, Wren squeezed his hand and muffled "Just a few more minutes."

Eliot laughed. Well, he had been correct, she needed the sleep. Now, how to wake her highness. Her head was leaning back on the car seat. It had to be uncomfortable, but she had snored most of the way. He had been tempted to record her. Instead, he had taken a quick pic with her mouth open.

Eliot leaned close and whispered, "Wren Bailey, if you do not wake up this moment, I'm going to lean over and kiss you in front of God and all your friends. 1-2-3 – ready or not?"

Wren's eyes popped open. What was going to happen in 1-2-3. She turned to look at Eliot. He was close. He was close to Wren's lips.

"I lied. I don't know how to count to five when it comes to you and even more so kissing you." Before Wren realized what was taking place, Eliot kissed her. His lips were warm. She inhaled. She was fully awake. Her lips betrayed her and opened for Eliot to taste the sweetness. Eliot nibbled at her bottom lip. He rubbed his thumb across the swollen lip. When he inhaled, he felt the desire that was coursing through his body in reaction to Wren and those lips. She had the most voluptuous lips he had ever seen. There is just no way he could stop at one kiss, but he also knew they had an audience.

He pulled back. "Wren Bailey, you're home!"

Wren tilted her head. She looked ahead and saw her mother and Kash. "Yes, we are. You ready to be interrogated and placed under the microscope, Mr. Mistletoe?"

Eliot could hear the worry in Wren's voice. "Wren, I was born ready. I'll answer all questions that might be addressed. Will the light be shining directly in my face?"

Wren could not stop laughing. She looked at Eliot and touched his arm, "I know you can handle them. Lights and all. Let's do this before they have any more time to think of additional questions for you."

Wren's mother watched the exchange between Mr. Mistletoe and her daughter. She could tell something had changed with her daughter. She knew just by the fact Wren was still sitting in the van and had not opened the door yet to greet her, Kash, and Wren's friends. Lynette was no stranger to that "look" between a man and a woman. Right now, that "look" was being displayed openly in that van.

Wren saw her mother out of the corner of her eye. No one had approached the van yet. It was if they were all waiting and holding their breath. Wren shook her head. They were so obvious. She reached for the van door to open and looked at Eliot. "Thank you."

Eliot grinned. "Wren, you're welcome. Come on, let's get started. I'm not leaving you. I'm here for the long haul." Eliot watched as Wren nodded in agreement and took the first step out of the van.

Chapter Eighteen

Kash was the first to greet Wren. Even Wren's mother could not squeeze in between the best friends. Kash whispered in Wren's ear. "My, my, Miss Bailey, you've been quite busy at the farm, haven't you?"

Wren hugged her friend tight. "Kash, trust me, you have no idea." With that one sentence, they both turned to look at who kept her busy. Eliot could feel their eyes on him. He walked towards them. He took the bull by the horns. Sometimes, it was best to address the elephant in the room, or as the case may be, the parking lot. "You must be Wren's best friend, Kash? It is a pleasure to meet you. Are we ready to unload the mistletoe for the event?"

"Wren told me you were a 'doer'. She needs someone like you," Kash stated.

Wren's mouth flew open. Her eyes were wide in disbelief. She turned to look at Kash. "I don't need anyone. I'm doing just fine by myself and with mother's help, of course."

Kash smiled. "Of course, you are." She winked at Eliot. "Always in control, this one."

Eliot shook his head. This best friend was a firecracker. He watched as Wren mouthed the words "Stop it." Wren looked at Eliot. She felt her cheeks blush. Would she ever feel normal around Eliot Mistletoe? Could she keep her attraction, especially her feelings, hidden from the rest of her friends, especially Kash?

Wren felt Eliot touch her elbow, and his lips were on the tip of her ear. "Where do we place the mistletoe, Wren? Just tell me what you want, and I will make it happen." He stepped back and smiled sheepishly. Wren pursed her lips together. She pointed her finger at him. "Eliot Mistletoe. Not now. I know that the mistletoe needs to go inside, where the kitchen is located. There is an industrial refrigerator that has been marked for storage. The mistletoe needs to remain cool until we are able to decorate for the wedding."

Eliot nodded. He reached for her pointing finger and began a circling motion around it. "You're right. I apologize. My thoughts were elsewhere, Wren. Just know, they're on hold for the moment. Until then, I await your command."

Wren's stomach tightened. This event/wedding had to go off without a hitch. And much to his chagrin, the hitch was standing in front of her, sexually arousing her. "I'll deal with the moment later. Right now, let's get the mistletoe stored." She turned away to find Kash. Kash gave her a thumbs up and began the instructions of what was necessary to take care of the mistletoe.

Watching as everyone chipped in, Wren felt different about this wedding. This would put The Polished Bannister on the radar of the elite of the elite brides planning their upcoming nuptials. There was no doubt in Wren's mind: this was the make-it-or-break-it event.

Eliot could not take his eyes off Wren. Wren was not bossy; she was demanding of perfection. With the help of all, the mistletoe had been safely stored in the refrigeration system at the church. He could not help but stare at Wren. She was beautiful. He had never met anyone like her. She was strong and determined. There was no doubt in his mind, and he did not want to admit, he felt something for Miss Wren Bailey. All Eliot could think about were those pouty lips. He knew she felt something. Every time he looked at her for longer than a mere second, her cheeks blushed light pink.

She would then turn away and begin another task or conversation with one of her friends.

He did not realize she was standing behind him until he heard her clear her throat. "Do not hurt her, Mr. Mistletoe. Wren and I have been friends since elementary school. There's no one else I trust more." Kash winked at Eliot to be sure he understood her exact meaning.

Eliot was about to reply that he would never hurt Wren, when she walked up to both he and Kash. "What are you talking about in such secrecy? Anything you would care to share with me?"

Eliot turned to see if Kash were going to respond. Kash laughed. "Believe it or not, I only gave him a warning. No threats, yet. I'm pretty sure Eliot and I are on the same page where it comes to you. Tomorrow is going to be the best one yet. I'm heading home. What time do you need me tomorrow?"

Wren chuckled. She was pretty sure Kash had said more, but it was late, and Wren needed to send everyone home, but not before giving them a return time. She motioned for all to come towards her. Eliot stood back and observed as they all came together. Wren thanked them and gave them the time to meet back tomorrow to begin the decorations for the wedding. He could not help but admire Wren and her determination with this little branch called mistletoe. The last car had left the parking lot. It was then that Eliot noticed.

Chapter Nineteen

Wren did a double check on the vehicles. All had left the church parking lot. It was finished. The mistletoe was stored safely. She hated to admit it, but she was tired. Between the drive down and back and then unloading and the event at the hotel with Eliot, Wren was spent. She was physically and mentally exhausted.

Wren had no clue when he had strolled towards her so quietly, but there he stood. He placed his finger under her chin. She did not want to look at him. She did not want him to see the desire in her eyes for his touch. It was just too much to absorb, and yet, she could not help herself.

"Wren, let's get you home. What do you say? I know you are beat. I've got to check in to the hotel. I can drive you home. You need to get some rest. I'll meet you here tomorrow at the time you gave to the others."

Before Wren could object or Eliot could add another word, they heard, "Excuse me, but you will do no such thing. There is no need in spending extra dollars, when we have plenty of room at our home. I will not take no for an answer. And Wren will not say anything. She's too tired to argue with her mother," Lynette stated as a matter of fact.

Eliot smiled. He liked Wren's mother. He could see a lot of Mrs. Bailey in Wren. "So long as Wren is okay with me staying in one of her beds, I am fine, Mrs. Bailey, and I appreciate your kindness."

He reached for the door-knob. ANOTHER DOOR KNOB! What was up with door knobs and Wren? Eliot hesitated. He looked down the hallway. She was watching him as well. Her hand was on her doorknob. He acknowledged her with a smile and a wink. He waited. She shook her head and grinned. He was incorrigible.

Sitting on the side of the bed, she knew she shouldn't. What if she heard her? What if he heard her? If she didn't do it now, she would never do it. She placed her feet on the floor and stood up. Wren opened her bedroom door and walked down the hallway. She was almost to his door, when it dawned on her, what was her story? Would he believe that she just wanted to be sure that his accommodations were to his satisfaction?

She raised her hand to knock, when she heard him inquire, "Whatcha doing, Miss Bailey?"

Wren turned so quickly she fell into his chest. "Easy now. You have a big event tomorrow. I do not need you injuring yourself. Can I help you with anything?"

Eliot knew she was caught. He also watched as her cheeks turned the ruddest red ever. Wren opened her mouth to respond. Nothing. She had nothing.

Eliot could not help but stare at Wren. She was biting her lower lip. He knew she was pondering her next move. He did not wait for her to decide. He pulled her into his arms. "Wren, do you have any idea what you are doing to me?"

Wren shook her head "no."

"Then let me show you, Wren." Eliot took his finger and traced the outline of her lips. He took his finger down the center of Wren's chin and followed to the center of her chest. He watched as Wren inhaled a breath and her breasts rose to his touch. Eliot took his thumb and index finger and began the trail around the curve of Wren's breast. Eliot could not take his eyes off Wren. He waited for her reaction.

Wren could not look at Eliot. She did not want him to stop, but she did not want him to know the effect he was having on her. Her emotions were already pensive. The drive, unloading the mistletoe, the hallway, and him. It was overwhelming, yet exhilarating. Wren had not felt this alive in a long time.

Without giving her time to realize the effect she was having on him, Eliot whispered in her ear, "I want you, Wren Bailey. Plain and simple."

Wren leaned into Eliot. He reached for her hand. Without missing a beat, Eliot pushed the door to his bedroom open. He reached for Wren's hand. He pulled her closer to his chest. "Wren, don't make me wait." Wren did not have the will nor desire to leave Eliot Mistletoe's embrace. He had a magical hold over her. She was not herself when she was around him.

"That was never my intention, Eliot Mistletoe." There was a lump in Wren's throat. Her heart was beating rapidly. Wren did not know where it came from. "I would like to kiss you without asking permission, but I do not know how. I shouldn't….."

Eliot grinned. "You just did. Come here." He swallowed hard. This woman, standing in front of him, asking for him to kiss her was going to send him over the edge.

Time stopped. Wren had never been this brazen before. Her heart pounded. Her knees grew weaker. Thank goodness he was holding her. The only thought in her mind was the softness of his lips against hers. She could not pull back. She did not want to pull back. He had invaded her world and now her senses. Was this a dream?

Eliot was totally taken back. She had caught him off guard. He had kept his eyes half open. He needed to be sure that Wren Bailey was not a figment of his imagination. She was wrapped in his arms and kissing him quite passionately.

Every breath he took smelled like mistletoe. She smelled like mistletoe. That small twig was proving to be mystical in nature. Eliot enveloped Wren's small frame with his arms and met her lips. "Wren, I cannot stop. I do not want to stop." Wren looked at Eliot. "I want you, Eliot. I need you."

He began to remove his shirt. He pulled it over his head. Wren watched. She could not look away. As he pulled the shirt away, his thick, short hair had become messy. From the moment she had made love the first time with Eliot Mistletoe, she had known there was an attraction. She did not want to think anymore.

He knew she was watching. "Do you like what you see, Wren?"

Wren felt the impulses in her spine as he pressed a little harder against her. Their cheeks brushed as they turned towards each other. Wren's eyes jumped from his eyes to his lips. It was such an adrenaline rush.

Pulsing warm sensations up and down Wren's body, Eliot's tongue conquered Wren's mouth. He was hungry for Wren. It was an all-consuming warmth pulling her into him.

Eliot pulled back. "Would you like me to kiss you again? This time I'm asking you, Wren."

It took less than a split second for Wren to give in. She surrendered to his lips pulling her under his spell. Wren did not want him to know. She did like being kissed. Eliot Mistletoe was a good kisser. She might even offer him the compliment of the word "great".

"Wren Bailey, do you have any idea of your powers over me when it comes to restraint. I'll be honest, I have none."

There was no hesitation. Eliot covered Wren's moist lips with his. He felt her shudder. Wren felt the change in Eliot and knew she was playing with fire, a second time. She heard the sound from the back of Eliot's throat. It was a half moan. She stopped thinking. There was no need to think but only to react. Little shivers of pleasure raced through Wren.

Eliot's hand reached for hers. He walked the few short steps to his bed guiding Wren. Eliot's hands slid around Wren's neck and he pulled her back to his mouth. It felt as if the room were spinning. Eliot began to remove Wren's clothing. Her pjs joined Eliot's on the floor. He did it with such ease. Wren stood before him. She felt the bed behind her legs. Eliot's hands were positioned on her back. "I have you, Wren. I will not let you fall."

Wren ran her fingers down Eliot's chest. Eliot followed the trail she had created. Wren had no idea what she was doing to him. Eliot could not allow any more hesitation.

Eliot needed to close the space between them. He lifted Wren up as she were made of air. She could only do what instinct told her. She wrapped her legs around Eliot's waist. Eliot's hands were cupping her. Wren whispered Eliot's name. "Promise me that something as thin as a piece of paper can never separate us. Always hold me like this, Eliot."

Eliot could not respond. He looked at Wren. "I promise, Wren. I will never let you go."

Eliot positioned Wren so that when he laid her down, the bed was right there, and so was he. Hiding himself within her warmth had never felt more right than now. As Wren pulled him closer, Eliot could no longer hold back. He ached for more. He was lost in her. Without a doubt, the world had ceased to exist. He knew he could never leave her.

Chapter Twenty

What had she done? How was she ever going to get through this event? Better yet, how was she going to get up from his bed without waking him. She only had a few hours to collect herself and begin the preparation for the largest wedding of the year.

Before she could question herself or waste additional time, he whispered near the back of her ear lobe, "Wren, I'm awake." She shivered. Lord, she hated the way her body responded to him. Betrayal was all she could think of. Every single time. There was no denying it any longer. Wren Bailey was attracted to Eliot Mistletoe, but there was another problem in this equation. Wren knew the attraction was there. The problem was her feelings for this man who had turned her entire holiday season upside down. It was like an invasion of two worlds.

"Wren, are you going to ignore me? I know how to get you to respond to me." Eliot trailed his hand down the silhouette of her naked body lying curled into his. He pulled her closer to his stomach, so she could feel him. He was aroused. She knew he was serious.

"No, I am not going to respond." Wren removed his hand from her hip. "You are not going to deter me from the task at hand. We have to get up and get moving. We both need to shower and then head to the church to begin the decorations inside and then straight to the venue for the reception." She turned to look at him and gave him a stern look.

Eliot chuckled. "Fine, you win. But there's always tonight. Do you want to shower in here or walk down the long hallway to your room as quiet as a feather floating to the floor?"

"Feathers and hallways," Wren grinned at him. "I'll take my chances. It's early. I don't think anyone is up and moving out of their rooms yet."

Eliot nodded from his bed. "Fine. I'll meet you downstairs as soon as I have showered."

Eliot watched Wren as she tried to inconspicuously poke her head out the door to check the hallway. She turned to look back at him. Something was wrong.

He did not want her to leave. He wanted her to stay. He wanted her to remain in the bed with him. Not for anything sexual but more conversational. He just wanted to talk to Wren Bailey. In the last few years, Eliot had not had the time to think of things like this – talking. . . .and especially with a woman in his bed.

No matter. This was not going to happen this morning. He was going to need that shower. After the event, before returning to the farm, he needed to talk to Wren. The feeling of needing another individual to make him happy was concerning for Eliot. Why now? Why her?

Chapter Twenty One

Arriving downstairs, he hardly recognized her. She was dressed all in black leggings, which in his opinion, were hugging her in all the right places. A black spaghetti tank and black jacket finished the ensemble. He knew she would have "killer" heels on. He was right. He smiled. They were black boots trimmed in fur around the lip of the boot. With designer sunglasses perched on head, designer bag in one hand, accessorized with jewelry, she was ready to take on the world.

Wren knew he was staring. She watched as his eyes moved from her black boots to her sunglasses on her head. When he stopped, he looked directly at her. Wren tilted her head and grinned. "Do you approve, Mr. Mistletoe?"

Eliot knew by her comment and the word "approve", she was teasing him. The tilt of her head and smile gave it away. Did he approve? He would like to show her how much he approved. Much later, that would happen much later. "Yes, Wren. You are in your element. You exude confidence, and as my dad would say 'just a bit of hoitety toitey' to top it off."

He then turned the tables. "So, do you approve of my wardrobe choices?"

Wren could not help but laugh. "Eliot, I do not think the word 'approve' even is in the sentence. You look quite charming. I'm sure not only my friends that you met last night will be under your spell, but the wedding guests, too. Yes, I approve."

Eliot could not help but pull her close to him. She smelled of peppermint lotion. He recognized that scent from their first time. If she were trying to entice him to take a nibble, it was working. "I know you are a bit anxious about this event, but it's going to be a success. You have so many supporting you, including me." Eliot kissed her. It was not a quick kiss. He wanted it to remain with Wren for the day. "Always, Wren Bailey, I will be here."

Wren could only nod a thank you. She had not expected that. Eliot Mistletoe certainly was full of surprises. His lips left hers. He stepped back. She stepped back. Wren was not a fan of the word "always".

Her father used to tell her the same thing. That was neither here nor now. In less than eight hours, her clients would walk down the aisle. There was still much to do.

Eliot placed his hand on the small of Wren's back. "Let's get going before I think of something much more fun to do than get scratched with the decoration of the prickly mistletoe."

Walking down the steps, Wren heard voices. Several of her crew had already arrived. Wren knew her mother had prepared breakfast. Both she and Eliot walked into the kitchen together. Everyone's eyes turned towards them. Kash clicked her tongue. "So, arriving together can only mean one thing. Everything okay with you two?"

Wren laughed. Kash was never one to beat around the bush. "Yes, Kash. We are both fine," Wren stated with conviction and looked at her friend with a glare, as to inform her not to say anything else. That wasn't the case.

"And, you, Mr. Mistletoe, is everything okay with you?" Kash asked with all the sweetness of a candy cane.

Eliot liked Kash. He also knew why Kash and Wren were such good friends. Both opposite in personalities, but each had a bit of mischievousness about them. "I'm just waiting to meet someone under that mistletoe. Do you have any suggestions?"

Before either could respond, Wren threw her hands high in the air. "Enough, both of you, enough. Let's eat and head to the church and venue. I've only enough energy to argue with one of you, and that's one at a time. I can't win with both of you," Wren smiled.

Chapter Twenty Two

Finally, they were at the destination. Wren had done hundreds of events. Why this one event was wreaking havoc on her nerves, she could not understand. The set up and time frame was the same as in previous weddings. Why did she feel like this event would be life changing for her?

Wren knew why. It was him. She wanted to impress him. She wanted him to feel a part of her world. She wanted him to be there. Something was changing. Something was off. That something was Eliot Mistletoe. Wren could not analyze herself. She was just too complicated for her own good.

Parking the van, Eliot looked over at her. Wren was pensive. Her brows were furrowed. He reached for Wren's hand laying on the van seat. "Hey, look at me. It's all here. Everything you need to make this a successful event is inside. We just need to set up. It's just like that commercial 'easy breezy'. I am not leaving you. I will be with you every step of the way. Okay?"

Wren saw it. He meant every word. She heard it in his voice. He genuinely cared about this event and her success. "If I forget to tell you, Eliot Mistletoe, I want you to know."

Eliot was never caught off guard, but in this moment, his entire world was surrounded by her words. She leaned her head into his and then *she* kissed *him*. Not the other way around. He had thought about it. She pulled back, and Wren told him before she chickened out, "I want you to know I'm glad you are here with me."

Wren opened the door. Eliot was still watching her. "You coming, or are you going to stare at me all day?"

Eliot winked at Wren. "I kind of like what I'm staring at, but urgency is required in this situation. Let's do this thing."

Standing in the back corner of the church, Wren could not help but pleased with the décor. It was elegant. It was beyond words. Poinsettias lined the pews from where the bride would enter until the first steps she would take to reach the groom. It was Christmas at its best.

Walking outside towards the reception venue, which was beside the church, Wren could see the entry to the doorway decorated in garland, bows, and white lights glistening. Alternating between red, white, and green, each window of the venue had a beautiful long-stemmed Christmas candle lit with vibrance. Wrapped around the candle, it had been positioned so as not to be right in your face, but to be seen as it was meant to be. It was a winter wonderland.

The long hallway to the main entrance was enhanced by the aroma of pine cones. At the end of the hallway before entering, each individual, couple, or family would be given the opportunity to have their pictures taken for memories for the bride and groom. Strategically placed above was the mistletoe. This would be where the tiny little branch with such significance would first be seen and begin the magic for the evening. This would be the first stop to receive the infamous mistletoe kiss.

Wren had no idea she had stopped directly under the mistletoe. She was perusing the room to be sure that the mistletoe had been positioned on every table. She inhaled deeply and smiled. Everything was falling into place.

Before she realized it, strong arms had slipped from behind and pulled her back to his chest. Time stood still.

Chapter Twenty Three

The wedding had concluded. All remarked of its beauty. The lighting, the music, the décor – everything had fallen into place like a fitted glove. She would have Kash and the team begin the clean-up. Wren did not want to look at the clock. Where had the day gone? The time had arrived. It was time to take Eliot to the airport. He needs to return – to his world. Eliot had loaded his luggage in the van before leaving for the venue that morning. Parking the van, they walked to his flight together. Silence. No words were exchanged between them. Approaching the bag check in, Eliot turned to grab the handle.

Wren placed her hand on top of his. "Don't go. Stay for an extended holiday. We have the room."

Eliot smiled. If only she knew his true feelings. "Stay." A word so easy to say and yet a word that would make such an impact. Timing was everything. "I cannot, Wren. I must return to the farm. I must help my dad close out the year. There is so much to do that he cannot do. If it were not the end of the year, who knows what I might say."

Wren shook her head. She understood. Time stood still for no one. Eliot leaned in and whispered in Wren's ear. "Just so you remember, I love you." Wren could not believe it. Did she hear him right? She stopped. Time had halted. She had not expected this. Wren watched as Eliot walked through the checkpoint. That was it.

She turned to walk back through the terminal and to return to the van. Wren could not leave just yet. She needed to let him know. He could not leave without her telling him. She was in love with Eliot Mistletoe. She ran back to the checkpoint. He was already through and probably loading onto the plane. Wren ran to the glass window. She could see it. Eliot's plane would soon be taking off. She could do nothing but watch. The airplane began taxiing down the runway in preparation for take-off. This is not how it is supposed to end. The plane lifted into the air. She tried to blink back a tear, but it escaped and slid down her cheek. The realization hit Wren. Eliot Mistletoe was gone.

Epilogue

Eliot's voice could not get any louder. He knew she heard him. He could hear the rustling of papers and a few expletives of "where the … did I place the paperwork?"

"Mrs. Mistletoe, if you do not shake your cute little berries and get a move on, we are going to be late to get to your mother's. Not only is she going to be ticked that you are late, but your best friend in the entire universe is going to be, as well. I can handle your mother, but can you handle your friend?"

She looked at him sideways. "Really, you can handle my mother? Absolutely, you cannot. Let me call her to inform her we are on our way and the approximate time we will arrive. As for my best friend, she cannot do anything without me. I'm the coordinator for her wedding."

Eliot walked towards her. "Wren Bailey Mistletoe, am I ever going to have a moment's rest with you?"

"No, you are not. You knew what you were getting into Eliot Mistletoe. Mother can wait. Kash can wait. Remember, you made that statement under the mistletoe, 'a kiss is *never* enough', and I concur that you are one hundred and ten percent correct. It is not. It will never be enough. I want more. I want you. Kisses until our last dying breath."

Eliot smiled. He would kiss Mrs. Wren Bailey Mistletoe as many times as she needed and wanted. He hated to admit when she was right. She was one hundred and ten percent accurate that "a kiss is *never* enough."

www.ingramcontent.com/pod-product-compliance
Lightning Source LLC
LaVergne TN
LVHW011846060526
838200LV00054B/4192